Let's Go Blue!

Aimee Aryal

Illustrated by Gerry Perez

www.mascotbooks.com

It was a beautiful fall day at the University of Michigan.

Two little Michigan fans were on
their way to watch a football game.
Let's follow them to the Big House!

The little fans walked onto the Diag.

Some students walking by yelled,
"Let's Go Blue!"

The little fans walked past classroom
buildings and passed in front
of the "UGLI."

A librarian coming out of the building
waved and said, "Let's Go Blue!"

The little fans walked through
the Law Quad.

A professor passing by said,
"Let's Go Blue!"

The little fans walked by the
Michigan Union.

Some older Michigan fans standing
outside shouted, "Let's Go Blue!"

It was almost time for the football game.
As the little fans walked to the stadium,
they passed by some alumni.

The alumni remembered going to games
at the Big House when they went to
U of M. They yelled, "Let's Go Blue!"

Finally, the little fans
arrived at Michigan Stadium.

They watched the football players
run onto the field. The crowd yelled,
"Let's Go Blue!"

The little fans watched the game from the stands and cheered for the team.

The Wolverines scored six points!
The quarterback shouted,
"Touchdown Michigan!"

At half-time the Michigan Marching Band performed on the field.

The little fans watched the band
form the Michigan M and sang,
"Hail to the Victors."

The Michigan Wolverines won
the football game!

The little fans gave Coach Carr
a high-five. The coach said,
"Great game Michigan!"

After the football game, the little fans were tired. It had been a long day at the University of Michigan.

The little fans walked to their homes
and climbed into their beds.
"Goodnight little Michigan fans."

For Anna and Maya, and all
little Michigan fans. ~ AA

Para mi abuela y abuelo, tia Margie, y tio Jose. ~ GP

Special thanks to:
Kristen Ablauf
Lloyd Carr
Chris Paulen
Dave Schueler
Kathleen Stevens

ALUMNI ASSOCIATION
UNIVERSITY OF MICHIGAN

The Alumni Association of the University of Michigan is an independent organization that nurtures lifelong relationships with and among current and future Michigan alumni. As a committed partner of the University, the Association offers programs of relevance and service to alumni and creates support for the University. We strive to be first and best for our 108,000 members—and all Michigan alumni. To join the Alumni Association, visit www.umalumni.com or call 800.847.4764.

Copyright © 2004 by Mascot Books, Inc. All rights reserved.
No part of this book may be reproduced by any means.

For information please contact Mascot Books,
P.O. Box 220157, Chantilly, VA 20153-0157.

THE UNIVERSITY OF MICHIGAN, MICHIGAN, UM, WOLVERINES, MICHIGAN WOLVERINES, U of M, GO BLUE, LET'S GO BLUE, "HAIL TO THE VICTORS," MICHIGAN STADIUM, BIG HOUSE, BLOCK M are trademarks or registered trademarks of the University of Michigan and are used under license.

ISBN: 1-932888-19-5

Printed in the United States.

www.mascotbooks.com